FAVORITE FABLES

RETOLD BY AMANDA ATHA

- ILLUSTRATED BY -

JANE HARVEY

BRACKEN BOOKS
LONDON

This book was first published in 1987 by Bracken Books
a division of Bestseller Publications Ltd
Princess House, 50 Eastcastle Street
London W1N 7AP, England

World Copyright, Text & Illustrations © Bracken Books, 1987

ISBN 1 85170 108 7

Printed and bound by Times Printers, Singapore

Contents

A Peacock and a Crane

A PEACOCK and a crane were talking together in a garden. The peacock was very pleased with his appearance and he spread out his tail to show the crane the full beauty of his feathers.

'My feathers are much finer than yours,' said the peacock. 'Look at the wonderful patterns they make.'

When he heard this boasting the crane sprang into the air and flew around and around above the peacock's head.

'Come and join me,' he taunted. 'It's much more fun flying around in the sky than being stuck on the ground the whole time. Your feathers are all very well but it seems to me they would be better still if they enabled you to fly.'

MORAL: *That which is useful is of more importance than that which is merely ornamental.*

The Hornets
and the Bees

One day some hornets found a piece of honeycomb. They pretended it was theirs, but the bees said: 'No, it's ours'. As they disagreed, they asked a wasp to act as judge for them in this matter. The judge was puzzled, because no one could prove anything. Some longish, brownish buzzing creatures had been seen near the comb, but that did not prove a thing. The trial went on and on for months and months and cost the litigants a lot of money.

At last a wise bee said: 'Enough is enough. We are wasting time, and money and honey is being wasted. Why don't we set to work and make *another* honeycomb, and then the whole world will see that *we* make the honey and not the hornets?'

The bees agreed to this, and soon the wasp judged that it was the bees who won the day.

MORAL: *Disagreements are better settled by common sense than by law and judges who cost a great deal of hard-earned money.*

The Hare
and the Tortoise

ONE day the hare and the tortoise were arguing over who was the best.

'Look at you,' said the hare contemptuously, 'you are dull and heavy and slow. You never get anywhere at all. I am light and gay and graceful. I can run farther in a few minutes than you can run in a whole day.'

'That is as may be,' replied the tortoise, 'but I will undertake to run a race with you for a wager.'

'How foolish of you,' said the hare, 'but if you want to be beaten, so be it.'

So they agreed a course and the fox said that he would be the judge. When the day of the race came they started together. The tortoise just kept jogging on at his usual pace and he was soon left far behind and out of sight by the hare, who gamboled along, waving to his friends and stopping to eat certain choice plants by the wayside.

However, the day was hot and after a particularly delicious carrot, the hare decided that he would lie down under a tree and have a short nap.

'After all,' he said to himself, 'I can overtake him in a couple of bounds whenever I please.'

However, the hare slept for longer than he meant. The tortoise plodded on past the hare and came to the winning post first, thereby gaining the prize.

MORAL: *Do not be overconfident: the best person does not necessarily win.*

A Dog and a Cockerel Go on a Journey

A DOG and a cockerel went on a journey together. At nights the dog slept in a hollow tree, while the cockerel roosted in the branches above him. At midnight, the cockerel used to crow 'cock-a-doodle-doo-oo', because that is what he used to do in the farmyard. One night a fox heard him, came to the tree and stood licking his lips at the thought of cockerel for supper. He tried to persuade the cock to come out of the tree: 'What a beautiful voice you have, how well you crow' he said, 'how I wish you would come down so I can shake you by the paw, to show how much I appreciate your fine music.'

'Of course I'll come down,' said the cockerel, 'just tell the doorkeeper below to open the door.'

The fox did so, and the dog, who was in the tree, promptly caught him.

MORAL: *Those who try to trick others are often tricked themselves.*

The Eagle
and the Rabbits

ONE DAY an eagle stole some baby rabbits to give to her eaglets to eat. The mother rabbit ran after the eagle, and begged her to have pity on her little ones and save them. But the eagle took no notice, and tore the baby rabbits to pieces. The mother rabbit, in grief and indignation, held a meeting of all the rabbits in her warren, and asked them to help her punish the cruel and savage bird. Now, it is not easy for small and fluffy rabbits to fight a huge and powerful bird like the eagle, but this is what they did. They all went together to the tree in which the eagle lived and nibbled away at the roots until the tree toppled over. All the eaglets fell out and a fox who was waiting below ate them up.

The mother rabbit was comforted by this, to think that although her children were dead, so were those of the eagle.

MORAL: *If many weak people join together, they can often beat one powerful person.*

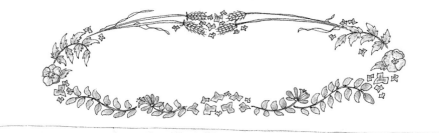

The Bear
and the Bees

ONCE UPON a time, a bear was stung by a bee. This made him so angry, he ran into the bee-garden and, without stopping to think, kicked over all the beehives in furious revenge. This made *all* the bees *very* angry as well, and they flew at him, and stung him in a thousand places and he wished he had never gone near them.

MORAL: *It is silly to pay someone back for one injury, if by doing so you make hundreds of enemies.*

The Fox
and the Grapes

THERE WAS a time when foxes were as fond of eating grapes as they are of eating lambs, and it was during this time that a fox who was *very* fond of grapes, happened to notice a bunch hanging on a vine. He stood underneath the vine and licked his lips at the thought of eating such a delicious treat. Then he tried to get them. He jumped and jumped and jumped, and tried a hundred times to get the grapes, but it was no good: he could not reach them. At last he gave up.

'Oh, bother the grapes,' he said, 'they are sour anyway.'

And off he went, pretending it did not matter.

MORAL: *It is easy to find an excuse for disappointment.*

A Wolf Turned Shepherd

ONCE UPON a time there was a crafty wolf who dressed himself up to look like a shepherd. He had a shepherd's crook, a shepherd's pipe, and he even walked and sat like a shepherd. In fact, he did it so well that once, in the dead of night, he started imitating the shepherd's voice and call as well. But this did not sound so shepherd-like. Indeed, it sounded so odd that the people round about took fright and attacked him, and he was so hampered by all his shepherd's clothes that he could not fight, and he could not escape.

MORAL: *Even the cleverest disguise may be found out.*

A Swallow
and a Spider

A SPIDER who was watching a swallow catch flies decided to make a web to catch swallows. 'Because,' she said, 'I am the one who catches things around here, not the swallow.'

So she spun a swallow-catching web. But the birds, without any difficulty, broke through her web and even flew away with it.

'Well,' said the spider, 'I can see that catching swallows is not one of my talents.'

So she went back to her old trade of catching flies again.

MORAL: *It is wise to learn by experience.*

An Oak
and a Willow

A<small>N OAK</small> and a willow tree were arguing about which of them was the strongest, the most reliable, and the most patient. The oak told the willow that the willow was weak and feeble, and let the wind push it about.

The willow said: 'Let us wait until the next storm comes along, and then we shall see who is strongest.'

Very soon after this there was a violent storm, and the wind blew and the rain streamed down. The willow, with its supple branches, blew this way and that, wherever the wind pushed it, and then bounced back, unhurt. But the oak was stiff and stubborn, and refused to bend until a terrible gust came and it broke.

M<small>ORAL</small>: *A wise man is prepared to give way so that he can live to fight another day.*

The Thrush
and the Jay

'WHEN WILL you build your nest?' said a thrush to a jay one fine day.

'Oh, by and by,' said the jay. 'It is so nice now that I want to hop and fly and sing while I can.'

'But you can sing while you work,' said the thrush. 'Look, I am gathering moss and twigs to make a nest, and while I work, I sing too. Listen.'

And she sang a fine song.

'Well,' said the jay, 'if you want to slave your life away, that is fine by me.' 'Well,' thought the thrush, 'if you *don't* build your nest it won't be fine for you.' But she said nothing, and the two birds proceeded to occupy themselves, each in her own way. The thrush hatched out five baby thrushes, and fed and sheltered them. The jay thought this dull work, but finally she threw a few sticks together, higgledy-piggledy, to make a nest, and laid her eggs in it, even though the nest was half finished.

One night there was a storm. The wind blew the jay's nest about and all her eggs fell out and broke on the ground. The jay was heartbroken, but the thrush and her little ones were safe and sound and had plenty of time to work, rest and play.

MORAL: *There is a proper time to work and a proper time to play.*

The Crab
and its Mother

A MOTHER crab said to her child: 'Don't walk sideways, dear, and don't drag your claws crossways over the wet rocks.'

'Mother,' said the baby crab, 'If you were to walk straight yourself, then I could walk behind and copy you.'

MORAL: *It is better to teach by example than by command.*

A Mountain and a Mouse

THERE WAS once a people who lived at the foot of a huge mountain. One day the mountain made a terrible noise, thundering and roaring, and the people were afraid, wondering what terrible monster was about to emerge. When at last the mountain opened to reveal the cause of all the roaring, there appeared not a terrible monster, as they had feared, but a tiny, ridiculous mouse.

MORAL: *An awful fuss is often made about nothing.*

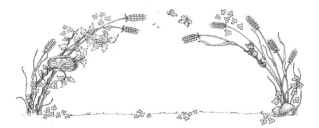

An Eagle and other Birds

Some birds were boasting among themselves: the hawk prided herself on her mighty wings; the crow, on her ability to see into the future; the nightingale boasted of her delicate singing; the peacock, of its beauty; the partridge, on its neatness; the wren, on its brave spirit; the duck, on its paddling, and the heron, on its supposed ability to prophesy the weather.

The eagle listened to all these boasts and said: 'This is all very well, but I have a sharp eye – let me carry one of you into the sky and I shall demonstrate my superiority.'

So the wren climbed onto the eagle, and the eagle soared into the sky and said: 'Can you tell what that speck is below?' The wren said she could not. 'It is a black sheep without a tail,' said the eagle, 'watch while I swoop to get it and eat it.'

And the eagle swooped, and fell straight into a trap.

'There,' said the wren, 'if only you had been as quick to spot the danger as you were to spot the sheep, you would have noticed the man setting up his trap near the sheep.'

MORAL: *Even the smartest person may be caught in a trap.*

A Swallow
and Other Birds

A FARMER was sowing flax. A swallow – which is a bird well known for its sense and foresight – called all the little birds together and said: 'Look what the farmer is doing. He is sowing flax, and flax is what traps and nets to snare us are made of. Go behind the farmer and pick up the seeds before they can start growing.'

But the birds took no notice, and the seeds took root and started to grow. Once again the swallows warned the birds of the dangers of flax, and told them it was still not too late to stop the damage. But once again, they took no notice, so the swallow said goodbye to her friends in the woods and went to live in the city. In due course the flax was harvested and woven into rope to make nets with. And the nets caught the birds – those very same birds whom the swallow had warned. The birds then realized how stupid they had been not to listen to the swallow, but it was too late: they were caught.

MORAL: *Fools will not believe in the effects of causes until it is too late to prevent them.*

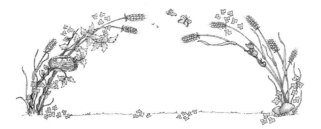

A Jackdaw
Borrows some Feathers

A JACKDAW wished to appear very grand, so he stole or borrowed all the fine feathers he could find and dressed himself up in them. And then he said: 'I am the grandest bird in the whole sky.' He was so puffed up with pride that his friends became jealous of him, and started to pluck out his borrowed feathers. And when every bird had plucked out a feather, the silly jackdaw had nothing left and sat there naked.

MORAL: *It is foolish to take pride in borrowed finery.*

Two Donkeys

Two donkeys were crossing the river. One was carrying salt, the other was carrying sponges. The donkey carrying the salt staggered under the weight of his burden, and fell into the water, but the water dissolved the salt so he soon got up again and went on his way feeling much better.

When the donkey carrying sponges saw how much more cheerful his companion appeared to be for the fall, he decided to follow his example, and he lay down in the river. But the water which had dissolved the salt sank into the sponges and made them forty times heavier, and the poor donkey drowned under their weight.

MORAL: *What is good in one case may be bad in another.*

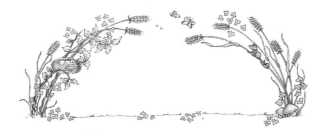

The Cat and the Mouse

ONE DAY a mouse saw a piece of bacon, and, while trying to get it, fell into the trap. A cat who was passing by saw the bacon and the prisoner and set about getting them both.

'Mouse,' he said, in a gentle wheedling voice, 'we have been enemies for so long that I am sick of it: let's be friends in future, do you agree? If so, I can help you.'

The mouse agreed most warmly to this. So the cat suggested that, as proof of their new friendship, the mouse should open the trap door so they could shake hands.

'By all means,' said the mouse. 'All you have to do is lift up that board by pulling down the long piece of wood which sticks out of it.'

The cat did so, and by doing so, opened the trap. The mouse scampered away into her hole with the bacon. The cat followed, but was too late: 'Well,' he said to comfort himself 'it doesn't really matter. The bacon was old and the mouse was very thin.'

MORAL: *Those who try to cheat often find they have been outwitted.*

An Ant
and a Pigeon

AN ANT was drinking at the side of a stream. Suddenly, she fell in. A wood pigeon who was flying past took pity on her, and threw her a little branch to catch hold of. The ant climbed on to the branch and so was saved from drowning. Soon after this, the ant noticed a man aiming a gun at the pigeon. Immediately she ran up to the man and stung him, so that he did not fire straight, and the pigeon flew away unhurt.

MORAL: *If you do a kind act, you may find yourself unexpectedly rewarded.*

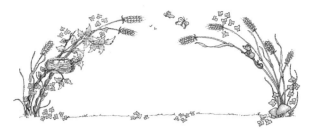

The Discontented Dog

A DOG saw a cat on top of a wall and said: 'I wish I could get up there. It must be nice to be so high. But I can't climb.'

And he was cross, and would not wag his tail. Then he came to a pond and said: 'How I wish I could live in a pond all day. Then I wouldn't be so hot.'

And he shut his eyes and lay down on the grass, while the fish in the pond wished they too could lie in the fresh green grass.

Soon he got up and went back along the road, and as he went he heard a bird say: 'I wish I could play all day long like that dog, and have a house made for me to live in. I have to fly to and fro all day, and my wings get so tired.'

And then, when he got back to the high wall, he heard the cat say: 'There goes that spoiled old dog, going home for his dinner. How I wish I was given meat as he is. I have had no food all day. How I wish I was like that dog.'

MORAL: *It is foolish to envy others, forgetting your own advantages.*

A Lion
and a Mouse

A MOUSE heard a beast roaring in the wood. She ran to see what the matter was and found a lion, stuck in a net. This reminded the mouse that she herself had been caught under the paw of a lion just a few days earlier, but the lion, being a very generous lion, had let her go free. It turned out that the lion in the net was the very same lion which had let her go, and so the mouse set to work immediately to gnaw through the threads of the net and let the lion go free, because she was grateful.

MORAL: *Little people who have been kindly treated may be of great help to powerful people in their hour of need.*

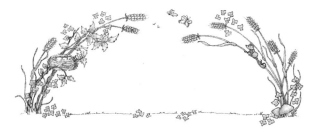

The Frogs
Choose a King

THERE WAS a time when the frogs had no king, but lived in the lakes in perfect freedom. They got tired of this though, and asked Jupiter, their god, to give them a king so that they could be ruled properly, with rewards and punishments. Jupiter listened, and threw a log into their lake to be king. It made a fearful splash and they were terrified and hid in the mud. Then one bold frog took a look at his new king, decided there was nothing to fear and jumped on top of him. And so did all the other frogs. Then they complained to Jupiter that this king was too boring and they wanted another. So Jupiter sent them another king in the shape of a great big stork, who took away their freedom and their possessions and attacked them. They complained again, but this time Jupiter sent back a message, saying: 'If you will not be content when all is going well, then you must be patient when things go wrong. You were better off with the log.'

MORAL: *If you change things just for the sake of changing them, you may well end up worse off.*

A Fox
and a Raven

A RAVEN was sitting in a tree with a delicious piece of meat in his beak. A fox saw it and his mouth watered and he immediately set about trying to get it for himself.

'Oh, beautiful bird,' said the fox, 'so graceful, so delightful and so well loved by everyone! What gorgeous plumes you have, and how *lucky* you are to be able to see into the future … If your singing is even half as good as all your other qualities, there cannot be another creature in the whole world so fabulous.'

The raven was flattered, and, to show that his voice was as beautiful as all the rest of him, he opened his beak and started singing so that the fox might hear him. But as he opened his beak, the piece of meat dropped out and the fox snapped it up.

'I spoke of your beauty,' said the fox, 'but you will notice I said nothing about your brains.'

MORAL: *Extravagant flatterers may be flattering in order to get something for themselves.*

[50]

The Eagle,
the Cat, and the Pig

AN EAGLE, a cat, and a pig lived in a tree together. The eagle nested at the top of the tree, the cat lived in the hollow trunk, and the pig lived at the bottom.

Now the cat was a troublemaker, and went telling tales to the eagle: 'You had better watch out,' she said, 'because the pig is always grubbing about at the bottom of the tree and one day she'll make it fall down, *then* where shall we be?'

And then, not content with that, she went to the pig and said: 'Just think what danger you are in. There's an eagle at the top of this tree and she is constantly watching your piglets, in the hopes of being able to eat them for her supper.'

The cat then went back to her kittens and guarded them by day and crept out at night to find food for her family. But the eagle did not dare move from her nest, for fear of the pig, and the pig did not dare leave her piglets for fear of the eagle. And so they both kept guard until they starved for lack of food, and left their children to the cat to take care of.

MORAL: *If you listen to tale-tellers, you will have no peace.*

The Dog
in the Manger

A CHURLISH, envious dog got into a manger, and lay there growling and snarling so that the horses could not eat the hay and oats which the farmer provided for them. The dog, of course, could not eat the hay himself, but he was so mean and nasty he preferred to risk starving himself rather than let anyone else benefit from the food he could not eat.

MORAL: *It is churlish and mean to stop other people using things which we cannot use ourselves.*

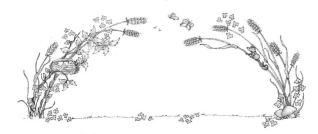